PERTARITO
KING OF THE LOMBARDS

Pertarito

King of the Lombards

by Pierre Corneille

Translated by John R. Pierce

John Pierce

Canton, Massachusetts

2020

ISBN-13: 978-1-7361151-0-7

John R. Pierce
https://twitter.com/jrpierce

TABLE OF CONTENTS

About *Pertarito* 2
Dramatis Personae 3
Act I 5
Act II 25
Act III 47
Act IV 67
Act V 86

About *Pertarito*

Pierre Corneille's play *Pertarito, King of the Lombards* (*Pertharite, roi des Lombards*), written in 1651, was given one performance in Corneille's lifetime. The critical reception was so negative that Corneille withdrew from writing for the theatre for several years. The play was published in 1653.

The action takes place in Milan in the seventh century. Pertarito, king of Milan, has been overthrown by a usurper, Grimoaldo, and is believed dead, though his death is not a certainty. Grimoaldo, who had promised to marry Pertarito's sister, Eduige, wishes instead to marry Pertarito's supposed widow, Rodelinda, the mother of Pertarito's son. Pertarito is discovered and brought to the royal court, but Grimoaldo treats him as an impostor.

Italian adaptations of Corneille's play were used as libretti for two operas in the eighteenth century, with Rodelinda as the title character, one by Giacomo Antonio Perti in 1710, and a more famous one by George Frideric Handel in 1725.

Dramatis personae

PERTARITO, king of the Lombards.

GRIMOALDO, Count of Benevento, having conquered the kingdom of the Lombards.

GARIBALDO, Duke of Turin.

UNULFO, Lombard lord.

RODELINDA, wife of Pertarito.

EDUIGE, sister of Pertarito.

SOLDIER.

The scene is at Milan.

Act I

ACT I. SCENE I.

RODELINDA, UNULFO.

RODELINDA.

The honor that he pays outrages me;
As I have said, for nothing will I change:
For me his conquests are but things to hate;
The homage that he shows renews my pain.
And as his love increases my torment,
As conqu'ror him I hate, as lover more,
And such I am, and such I wish to be.
That's what you're now to tell the count your boss.

UNULFO.

The king, Madame.

RODELINDA.

Indeed I do not think
Grimoaldo asks of me a heart so low:
If he loves me, he'll love my worthy pride
That risks my fortune and fulfills my birth.
If an unhappy king's sad flight and death
Give him security upon the throne,
The widow should not seem to treat as king
A prince who's king only as the result.
Let him not dare to hold so vain a hope:

For me he's always Benevento's count,
Always usurper of the sceptre he,
Always the author of our misery.
UNULFO.
That's not to know the source of all your woes,
To impute them to all that he has done.
Allow his virtue have what it is due,
For Pertarito is the one to blame:
It was his wish for more . . .
RODELINDA.
Do you forget
You speak to me of him who was my spouse?
UNULFO.
No, no, but you forget that although birth
Gave to the elder son the right to rule,
He nonetheless was made to share with him
A sceptre that his arm was to support;
Thus there were two kings in your Lombardy,
Two brothers: one Milan, one Pavia.
And Gundeberto, king of Pavia,
Wished all of Lombardy within his hands,
And could not stand to see his brother hold . . .
RODELINDA.
Say that 'gainst father's orders he rebelled.

The king who knew what each of them was worth,
Upon his deathbed gave to each a share:
Too kingly to him Pertarito seemed
Not to be left a kingly heritance:
And saw in Gundeberto one who seemed
Deserving not to be his brother's king.
It violates no rights of any crown
To try to hold the share a father gave;
It is to treat as law his final wish,
And to defend his choice to honor him.

UNULFO.

Since you so wish, his conduct I excuse;
Condemn at least the author of that plan,
Whose unwise love for his two kindly sons,
By making them both kings, undid them both.
Bad statesman he for failing to have seen
There can be but one master for a state.
Kings have a single throne and majesty,
Among their children there's no parity.
Birth has an order that's infallible,
That makes a crown be indivisible.

RODELINDA.

Yet by events has heaven shown to us
That it approved his honest sentiments.

And Gundeberto's jealous striving hate
Toward Pertarito found its penalty.
A battle 'twixt them emptied the discord:
Defeated, he was soon about to die:
His death would leave us all of Lombardy,
Of which he'd send to us the weaker part;
And tears I've shed that I would not have shed
Had Grimoaldo not meddled here at all.
He promised vengeance, and his stronger hand
Brought Gundeberto's hate to victory:
When we believed the sceptre in our grasp,
We changed our fate when we changed enemy.
To see him reign where the two brothers reigned,
To him I can impute our misery.
UNULFO.
Excuse a love extinguished by your eyes:
For Eduige his heart was then disposed;
To win the sister that he so desired,
The brother's passions did he have to wed.
'Twas more to conquer her he armed his troops
Than to do harm to you or help your foe.
Said to him Gundebert, about to die,
"As I approach the ending of my days,
You haven't brought your help to me in vain;

My death leaves you my sister and my feud:
If you dare love her, you will fight for her."
He names her queen, and then without delay
The chiefs and soldiers having sworn an oath,
He takes an oath from her and from the prince:
"To show to both how much I do love you,"
He said, "I give you Grimoaldo for spouse,
But on condition that he worthy be;
And, sister, you won't think he merits you,
Till he 'gainst Pertarito 's venged my death,
Conquered Milan and there imposed his rule.
To a queen's hand should be joined a king's."
And there is what he wished and what they swore,
And why the two opposed themselves to you.
Think not my prince, impatient in his love,
Wished to prevent fulfilling what he'd sworn;
But 'gainst his love the obstinate princess
Always opposed the word that she had pledged;
So well that lacking any other hope,
Incessantly he had to fight and win.
At last, after two years, Milan's conquest
Encrowned his head and gave Eduige to him.
If this Milan of which she'd been the prize
Had not lost to his eyes what they had won,

Another fate, another heart he found:
You were his captive, and you made him yours;
And then the princess, strange as it may be,
Wanting a king, then lost him totally.
We saw him turn his thoughts away from her,
No longer have a pressing urge to wed,
Avoid Eduige, and hardly speak to her,
Retreat from her upon diverse pretexts.
And for some time he has tried to snuff out
A fire of which your virtues could complain;
So long as you'd a fleeing spouse alive,
No more the sister's, he dared not be yours;
But when his death had made legitimate
That ardor that had been till then sweet crime . . .

SCENE II.

RODELINDA, EDUIGE, UNULFO.

EDUIGE.

Madame, if I were of a jealous sort,
I'd be annoyed to see him here with you.
And I should think, what very well may be,
This faithful agent's speaking for his boss;
But since my spirit's not so indiscreet
As to wish you disclose a secret sweet,

From such opinion I shall stay away,
To place within your choice what I should take,
Follow your rule, believe with great respect
What you may wish of interview suspect.
RODELINDA.
The secret's not so great that one can't guess,
And one can think whatever one may think.
Yes, ma'am, his boss's eyes are very bad;
And, yes, he could put them to better use.
EDUIGE.
Oh, he may marvel when he looks at you,
And he'll escape you if you don't watch out.
One needs obey him, though he lover be,
And want whate'er he wants, just as he want.
RODELINDA.
Have you seen in your own experience
One must defer to his disquietude?
EDUIGE.
You know only too well what his word's worth.
RODELINDA.
"Tis one thing to be count, another king;
And as a change in rank renews a soul,
From disloyal count comes faithful king.

EDUIGE.

But sometimes, Madam, with facility
One thinks a husband dead who's full of health;
And when one's getting set to wed again,
The husband can come back surprisingly.

RODELINDA.

What have you seen or have you heard, Madame?

EDUIGE.

Perhaps all that alarms a bit too soon.
It's not of Pertarito that I speak;
But still it's possible that he revive,
And give to your desires their rightful lord;
And as a sister I give this advice.

RODELINDA.

Do not abuse the name your pride rejects.
If you were sister, you'd be my subject;
A sceptre is worth more than ties of blood,
And nature cedes its place to splendid rank.

EDUIGE.

The news frets you, or at least importunes
The hope of a good fortune that you've formed.
Console yourself; there may be nothing to't;
And often one knows not of what one speaks.

RODELINDA.

He knows nothing, whoever makes you think
That I find glory in Grimoaldo's fires.
He's valiant and he reigns as one should reign;
But all his virtues leave me with disdain.
I hate the valor that's brought him the crown;
I hate the goodness that's won hearts for him;
I hate the prudence that beguiles some folk;
I hate the justice that engenders love;
I hate the plan to insure what he's won
By joining my crown firmly to his head;
I hate him all the more the less I see
How to undo someone who reigns with love.

EDUIGE.

This hatred that his virtue makes for you
Ingeniously shows you his good points;
And one who so speaks of a hated man
Might yet speak ill of him if he did please.

RODELINDA.

A brute who hates gives full rein to his hate:
He throws himself where'er his fury leads.
Only false portraits does he wish to see;
But he who hates by duty will see straight;
His reason rules and it is always fair,

And sees the good the hated one may have,
And would see in a loved one things to blame,
If that same duty ordered him to love.

EDUIGE.

You know of it a lot.

RODELINDA.

And how to live.

EDUIGE.

You thus provide a model one should match.

RODELINDA.

To live a sane life one should act like me.

EDUIGE.

And one who wishes love should speak to you?

RODELINDA.

I love your hint of punishment of self:
If it insults, it then sees its own guilt.

EDUIGE.

What? You'd refuse Grimoaldo as your spouse?

RODELINDA.

If I accept him, would you try to thwart?
Whatever rouses in you such alarm,
As soon as I like him, will cost you tears;
Whatever pow'r you think you have o'er me,
A word from me will be a law for you.

Seek not to go, Madame, where I lay claim:
His heart is wholly mine, should I wish it.
Console yourself: his offer's made to me in vain;
I want his crown, but do not want his hand.
Revive my husband if indeed you can,
That he oppose the love that bothers you.
Produce a ghost or spread an untrue tale,
To gain again the prince who's fled from you;
I'll help your ruse, and do whate'er I can
To fool with you the so triumphant prince,
To send to you the vows he's offered me,
And have no more annoyances to bear.
EDUIGE.
One who thinks I made up such a tale
Might not be pleased to find that it is true,
And far from truly helping out the ruse,
Just might refuse to see reality.
RODELINDA.
Oh, after robbing me of spouse and crown,
To take my glory 'd be to go too far,
By adding infamy to such rough blows.
Now know me, Madam, disabuse yourself.
I shall not hide, having a royal soul,
For love of sceptre I'll contend with you,

And I can't see with weak and yielding heart
My husband's sister dispossess my son;
But in my sad days never do I think
Of ending them by union with their cause,
To mount again the throne, the throne I want,
By marriage to the author of my woes!
No, wrongly you presume that I am set
To let my hand become a thing of his:
Unulfo can tell you, as he has seen,
With how much art and care my hand is sought.
And if despite the past exchange of vows,
He ceased to care for you when he'd seen me,
My feelings for the ashes of a spouse
Give him the scorn that you receive from him.

SCENE III.

GRIMOALDO, RODELINDA, EDUIGE, GARIBALDO, UNULFO.

RODELINDA.

Come, Grimoaldo, and tell this jealous one,
To whom at least you owe the name of wife,
If ever since I've seen you sigh for me,
I've ever with a wink given you hope;
Or if you want to leave eternally

This anxious one a thing to fear in vain,
Tell me my husband's deplorable fate:
He lives, he lives, if her report is true;
The grand pomposity of fun'ral rites
Were but illusions with which you tricked me;
And the rich tomb his conqu'ror made for him
Is but a charm to win over my heart.

GRIMOALDO.

Madame, you know what has been told to me,
That traveling abroad from place to place,
To ask for help 'gainst Eduige and me,
He met his end when with the king of Huns;
And if since he's been dead I've tried to say . . .

RODELINDA.

You must not wait for anything from me.
I owe his memory, myself, my son,
What I owed to the knots that held us close.
To vengeance only does my heart pay heed;
And since my heart must now explain itself,
If ever from your hands I make escape,
Then I shall carry my just plans with me:
I'll trace his steps to both ends of the earth
To find some foes to take up war 'gainst you;
Or if I languish captive in Milan,

I'll pray for vengeance from heaven above.
And will not stop till thunder from the skies
Disintegrates your head on stolen throne.
Madame, you see now with what sentiments
I make an obstacle to what you seek.
Goodbye: and if you can, preserve my throne,
Regain also the heart I leave to you.

SCENE IV.

GRIMOALDO, EDUIGE, GARIBALDO, UNULFO.

GRIMOALDO.

What have you said and what do you suppose
To make her doubt the end her husband's met?
Since when, from whom, do you know that he lives?

EDUIGE.

The confidant so dear will tell you too.

GRIMOALDO.

Will you have said that I have feigned his death?

EDUIGE.

Be not alarmed, for she believes me not.
Her future's softer as widow than wife,
And you have too much asked she deem him dead.

GRIMOALDO.
But then?
EDUIGE.
But then, each one knows what he knows;
And when it's time we'll see what's the effect.
Now wed her, traitor, make her infamous:
Who rapes a state can also rape a wife;
Adultery and rape are tyrants' rights.
GRIMOALDO.
You formerly did call me something else.
When I was winning battles to gain you,
When my arm shook with thunder Milan's walls,
When fright and terror I sowed everywhere,
I was a hero and a worthy king;
But since I rule as a greathearted prince,
Who values virtue and punishes crime,
And people see their lives improve 'neath me,
I'm but a tyrant, since I love elsewhere.
No longer is it valor or high birth
That gives to one the right to rule a state:
It is your love alone that makes conqu'rors
Be kings or tyrants, insofar as yours.
And if displeasing you confers bad name,
I simply must love you to shake it off;

And in an instant from usurper foul
To a true king my love for you will change.
EDUIGE.
Claim not my love after your perfidy.
I've put within your hands all Lombardy;
But do not blind yourself with your new care:
It's only 'neath my name that you reign here.
The people soon will show you by their hate
That they adored in you their queen's beloved,
That they respected her and want no king
Who has begun to break his faith with her.
GRIMOALDO.
If you were now in Pavia, Madame,
Where you by your late brother were named queen,
Your speech, although somewhat unseas'nable,
Could have at least some scintilla of sense.
But here in Milan, site of my conquest,
Where my boldness alone has crowned my head,
Amidst a state where all the people, mine,
Would fear you only as the king's beloved,
Your threat so powerless is of bad grace:
With weakness such the voice should be kept low.
I reign here, and shall reign despite your spite;

I act as judge for all, and even you.

EDUIGE.

For me?

GRIMOALDO.

For you, Madame.

EDUIGE.

After our pledge!

After two years of love so foully left!

GRIMOALDO.

No, two years of hatred, two years of scorn,

Which for all my flame are the sole prize.

EDUIGE.

Do you call scorn a friendship that's sincere?

GRIMOALDO.

A friendship faithful to fraternal hate,

A long pride armed with frivolous contract,

In order to oppose a lover's joy.

If you had loved, you'd not have been ashamed

To share with valiant count your destiny.

Refusing to be his till he was king,

That was to sell and not to give yourself.

I made myself a king to please your will:

At risk of my own life I won your heart;

But now that it's my due, I see I'm free

To leave you a good I bought too dear,
And your ambition's punishment is just
When from your tyranny I free a king.
A king must power have, and I'm no king
If I am not allowed to rule myself.
'Twould be abandonment of royal rights
If on the throne I were a slave myself;
And on this throne where you wished me to be,
I must rule o'er myself as over all:
It's the prize for my blood, let me have it,
And blame only yourself for what I'll do.
EDUIGE.
From conqueror so great a bad defense!
How very strange a king you make yourself!
Don't say your rank requires you leave me,
Or that betrayal is a royal right;
But if you would betray, then find, ingrate,
Excuses based on interests of state.
Say that a usurper must please the hate
Of his subjects by marrying their queen;
Making them think he'll render to her son
A sceptre that he conquered unjustly;
That for the son's minority he'll rule,
And would hold power in a sort of trust,

That he seeks for himself no other roles
Than spouse of queen and tutor of the king;
And say that otherwise you would lose pow'r,
That love of former kings would undermine;
Say that a tyrant who's 'midst enemies
Has need of such a plan to keep the throne.
The plausible appearance you'd create
Might make your cowardice less visible;
And thus could be attributed to need
What is but volatility's effect.

GRIMOALDO.

I welcome good advice, from whence it come.
Unulfo, go and find again the queen,
And with this offer try to win her o'er.
Madame, 'twill be to you I'll owe her heart;
And to revenge myself, I will take care
To choose for you a spouse who will love you,
Someone worthy of you, and worthy of
The love that you had wished to give to me.

EDUIGE.

O traitor, I want what your death gives me,
The one who strengthens by your blood my crown.

GRIMOALDO.

You easily could find someone for that.

Accompany the princess to her suite,
Duke; and try to crush a plot against my life
That I should fear were I in Pavia.
EDUIGE.
Fear me, in Pavia or in Milan.
To slay a tyrant ev'ry place is fit;
And you've no place to find security,
If I'm the prize for one who spills your blood.
GRIMOALDO.
Dissimulate at least such raging thoughts:
A tyrant I shall be, but just for you.
EDUIGE.
I've not a craven heart that would pretend.
GRIMOALDO.
Go then, and fear if you would make me fear.

Act II

ACT II. SCENE I.

EDUIGE, GARIBALDO.

EDUIGE.

I've told the traitor, and I say to you:

I owe myself this joy after such scorn;

And my great wish for punishment for him

Assures the punisher is to win me.

Pursue the path of my deservèd rage

And thus you will obtain me for yourself.

To win my love one must respect my hate:

The prizes are the sceptre and a queen;

Grimoaldo punished makes worthy of me

Whoever dares to love me, to be king.

GARIBALDO.

To set such price for your self and your crown,

Is not to know your hatred and yourself;

He who with such a hope would obey you,

Would be making himself object of hate.

The fickle Grimoaldo does not charm you,

But punished Grimoaldo would cost you tears.

The pity that you'd feel when his blood flows
Would soon revive past feelings of good will,
And his guilt, then extinguished with his life,
Would pass to him who'd acted to serve you.
Despite his scorn, imagine now his death,
And see your heart will not agree with it.
Whatever be his volatility,
It's vile, but his person still is dear;
In vain one takes apart what love has joined,
A sigh is what one needs to put it back.
Thus hope not that one ever can be sure
About the feelings that the falsehood took.
If anger at his volatility
Demands a vengeance with sincerity,
Then to the worthy hands you call upon,
You'd need be present, not a future, gift,
To join your destiny, with name of spouse,
Unto the arm that then will act for you.
So long as dubious may seem the prize,
Would one dare punish his disloyalty?
Your trembling hate a bad support would be

To one who'd undertake the task for you;
Whate'er sweet hope is offered by your ire,
A stronger hate would be the salary.
So give yourself, Madame; the venger then
Would have no need to dread a change of heart.

EDUIGE.

How hard you are in favor of a cheat
To wish to read to the depths of my soul,
Where my forsaken love, I sadly quell,
Becomes a secret party 'gainst my hate!
Whatever judgments that my mouth pronounce,
Are vain attempts my heart might then renounce.
This coward would shield me despite myself,
And wants to die from the avenging blow.
Avenge me then, but in another way:
And to preserve my life, let him have his.
Whatever death to his falseness I owe,
Take Rodelinda from him, that's enough;
Cause her to love elsewhere; punish his crime
With a despair that's similar to mine.
Do more: if it is true I've pow'r o'er you,

Then bring that ingrate trembling to my knees,
The heart repentant, tears upon the face,
Apologize in full for craven acts,
Beseech the pardon that he merits not,
And place within my hands his life and death.

GARIBALDO.

Add to it, Madame, although in your eyes
This hateful hand pierce heart that loves you still.
And though the faithful lover, killed on whim,
Expire in the stead of what he'd breached.
Less rough will be the order, less the pain,
Than what your injustice prescribes for me:
And death in self has naught so rigorous
To equal making rival happier.

EDUIGE.

Duke, you alarm yourself, not knowing me:
To love a traitor my heart's not so low.
I wish that he repent, repent in vain,
To render hate for hate, and scorn for scorn;
I wish his soul, the slave of mine, in vain
Ask for my grace, and never it obtain,

SCENE II.

GARIBALDO.

Oh, what confusion! And what tyranny
Tells me to hope for what she would deny!
And in what way is it to heed one's vows
To make a lover go to work 'gainst them?
Oh, make no claim, on such a slender hope,
That I'll try to return a heart I steal.
I love you, but I love self even more.
It's I alone who caused unfaithfulness;
It's I alone who turned him toward the queen:
And I will not destroy the work I've done.
For you he chose me, lest another spouse
Embrace your anger with too great a warmth;
But, yes, he fools himself by choosing me.
I love you much, but more I love the crown;
My aspiration that tries to win you
Wants from the marriage just the right to rule.
With your resentments, if there be the need,
I'll join a hundred hatreds to your own,
Create him tyrant by my own advice,

Set up devices to add to his loss,
And mix a little boldness in my speech,
To set the stage for me to take his place;
As marriage then will give me rights o'er you,
I shall marry you, to become king.
But here is Grimoaldo.

SCENE III.

GRIMOALDO, GARIBALDO.

GRIMOALDO.

Oh, well! What hope,
Duke? And what have we gotten from your work?

GARIBALDO.

Lord, order me no more to worship her,
Or do not leave her any cause for hope.

GRIMOALDO.

What? I had irritated her so much
To make your flame be better heard by her,
So that her spite and feelings against me
Would make her more receptive to your words,
And with the warmth that she would feel for you

She'd place within your hands her ball of hate:
And yet the hope she has to get my throne
Cannot by all our cares be torn away!
But have you promised you'd give her my head?
Have you not made the offer carelessly,
With coldness that could lead her to suspect
That really you did not wish to comply?

GARIBALDO.

No, nothing I forgot that could produce
A true resentful wish to undo you;
But her true feelings cannot be disguised:
Her ardent anger burns to be appeased;
And I won't get her, lord, to hear from me,
Till she has seen your marriage beyond doubt,
And till, with Rodelinda your dear wife,
You've chased from her heart hope of being yours.

GRIMOALDO.

Alas, in vain I set these plans in use:
No prayers nor vows are weakening her will.
Despite my efforts, day by day I see
Both her resistance and my love increase;

And if Unulfo's offer moves her not,

If the thoughts of her son don't soften her,

Henceforth I will no more try to persuade

A heart whose pride my efforts have increased.

GARIBALDO.

No, no, my lord, that pride must cede to you;

And a strong sickness needs a kindred cure.

Just show yourself as lover and as king;

Know how to order if in vain you ask.

What use is power that comes with a crown

Unless a king employs itself for himself?

A king's no less a king for being charmed,

And needs to make obey one who won't love.

GRIMOALDO.

To tyrants bring your maxims damnable:

I hate the ruler's art that warrants crime.

Now what example would I show today

If I'd arrest all those who'd do the same?

No great advantage has the pow'r of kings

For which king's conscience must not make account.

And love is no excuse for unjust reign;

A lover king must as a lover act.

GARIBALDO.

Now if you won't use force, at least use fear;

For happiness deign to constrain yourself;

And if Unulfo's offer's met with scorn,

Then make a threat against her young son's life.

GRIMOALDO.

So foul a deed to satisfy myself!

GARIBALDO.

If you do not dare speak, then let us act:

We will serve you, my lord, despite yourself.

Lend us only a moment of your ire,

And then let one explain or let one feign

To make her fear what you would dare not say.

You'll deny all. For after such events

Kings can deceive, and without punishment.

GRIMOALDO.

Let's hear Unulfo out 'fore we decide

If I'll place in your hands that thunderbolt.

SCENE IV.

GRIMOALDO, GARIBALDO, UNULFO.

GRIMOALDO.

What news, Unulfo? Is it time to die?

Have you seen for your king no hope to cure?

UNULFO.

More sensible seems Rodelinda now,

Apparently with less relentless pride,

She listened to me with tranquility . . .

GRIMOALDO.

But did she acquiesce? Did you move her?

Did she show joy? Did she seem moved at all?

Will she consent to tolerate my sight?

What did she say?

UNULFO.

A lot, but nothing clear:

She peacefully allowed the interview;

She seemed somewhat surprised, but tranquilly . . .

GRIMOALDO.

Oh! You are killing me with useless talk:

I do not care about tranquility;
Just tell me what she will agree to do.
When does she wish I give her son my crown?

UNULFO.

She wishes to reply to you herself.

GRIMOALDO.

What then? To nothing did you pin her down?

UNULFO.

It should be clear to one who can discern:
You'll never have a clearer form of proof.
Who asks to see you, can't wish to displease;
Refusal would have been explained to me,
Without requesting presence of the king.

GRIMOALDO.

And what about the spouse Eduige revives?

UNULFO.

For such a rumor she has scant belief:
So heavy seems the hoax it can't move her.
From one so suspect it can have no pow'r.

GARIBALDO.

Eduige herself seems little to believe

The story that she enjoys telling you;
It's just a falsehood she wished to create
To agitate the queen and you, my lord.
But I see Rodelinda comes here now.

GRIMOALDO.

I hear my sentence though it be not said:
I'm going to die, Unulfo, and your zeal
Has tricked you first and also has tricked me.

UNULFO.

Have hope, my lord.

GRIMOALDO.

You wish, and so I hope.
How bitter will become tranquility!
The little hope that I can get from you
Will render rough the blows about to fall!

SCENE V.

GRIMOALDO, RODELINDA, GARIBALDO, UNULFO.

GRIMOALDO.

It's true your soul so sensitive, Madame,

Now seems disposed to be compassionate;

May sweetness and esteem within your heart

Replace all hatred and all thought of scorn,

And may once hidden kindness guide your steps

Instead of the disdain shown heretofore.

RODELINDA.

That heart is now surprised by such complaints:

Count, never did I have disdain for you;

My hatred would have thought it was a crime

To lessen the esteem that's owed to you.

When I can see your conduct in my states

Win o'er the hearts to the work you've achieved,

With those hearts that your skill has gotten you,

I say that in your person virtue reigns;

With them I praise you, and with them I doubt

That they'd be happier with their true king:

These high virtues on which your power rests
Make up for what may lack as to your birth!
But whatever's been seen that is so grand,
I'm surprised by what Unulfo said.
A conqu'ror on the throne, and one who's loved,
Rules justly over all and over self!
He thinks that he usurps the throne he's won!
What he takes from the father, he'd give son!
It's an attempt to weaken the prestige
Of the most famous names in history,
That great Augustus, though he'd dared to try,
Did not dare fully carry out the plan.
And so I come to give you my reply,
To give you for my son . . .

GRIMOALDO.

Ah! Madam, stop;
No need to low'r yourself to give me thanks:
It's I who owe you all; and if my thoughts . . .

RODELINDA.

Allow my thoughts, please, and let me now put
In perspective that plan of yours so great,

And let my own hand try to take away
The impure mix with which you would stain it;
For finally the effort's nature's such
That its source to our eyes must be all pure:
Great virtue must reign in so great a plan,
And be its cause, and honor be its goal;
And since it would be soiled by hope of gain,
Or by chagrin of love, or wish to please,
It must have no defeated bravery,
Where passion and not virtue's seen to reign.
O count, consider well; for loving me,
Imprint not any stain on such a tale;
Believe your virtue: let it act alone,
Lest such an effort give you cause to blush.
They'd say of you then that a woman'e eyes
Had moved your soul more than your glory had;
They'd say the hero, of such great renown,
Would be a tyrant if he had not loved.

GRIMOALDO.

Give me that shame, I'll take in glory's place:
Make of your scorn my final victory.

Let them impute to my so happy arm
That only for your love 'twas generous.
And let this love, by effort oh so just,
Impair Augustus' great name and high deeds,
That it have more pow'r than its virtues had.
This wondrous plan is of nature such
That it would not spring from a purer source;
And no affection of the noblest sort
Could stain great deeds at all in any way.

RODELINDA.

Count, what you plan throws dust into your eyes
And leaves them then incapable of sight.
On such conditions to give back the throne,
Enslaves the mother while it crowns the son;
And it would not be so much to give back
As to sell, my honor as the price.
Your glory then would grow, just as you wish;
But mine would fade into obscurity.
What be your love, what be your worthiness,
Dear Pertarito's fall and then his death,
Which sketch in bloody way your own high deeds,

Depict them then as losses in my eyes;
And seeing them with the eyes of a foe,
With infamy would I take part in them.
And these are feelings I cannot betray:
I must esteem you, but must also hate;
I must act as a widow, after all,
And bear the hate as much as the esteem.

GRIMOALDO.

Ah! Bring yourself to see in kinder terms
The crimes that made me worthy now of you:
Through them my valor at an army's head
Gained me the fame of heroes of the past:
Through them I conquered, and through them I've reigned,
Through them my fairness won so many hearts,
Through them alone I'm worthy of the crown,
Through them I see you and see you with love,
Through them at last my very perfect love
Dares do for you what never has been done.

RODELINDA.

You do it for yourself, as recompense;

Again I say that all your valiant deeds,

Which made you seem a criminal to me,

Forever place an obstacle 'tween us.

So keep your conquest, and leave me my name:

Respect a husband's memory and shade:

You drove him from the throne but not my heart.

GRIMOALDO.

Unulfo, that's the softness you spoke of!

It's thus her soul, more reas'nable at last,

Seems to have overcome her so great pride!

GARIBALDO.

My lord, recall that now it's time to speak.

GRIMOALDO.

Oh yes, too great to hide is this insult:

She will be punished, and since she shows scorn,

I will become a tyrant over her,

And will not let her undeservèd pride

Mock more my kindness with impunity.

RODELINDA.

Become a tyrant then: renounce esteem;

Renounce your fame for magnanimity . . .

GRIMOALDO.

Revenge is sweeter than those names so vain;

If they can bring no joy, what good are they?

It's justice that I tame one who defies.

One who won't rule deserves to be a slave.

Go now, without arousing more my ire,

Await whate'er your master will command.

RODELINDA.

Who fears not death fears not what you'll command.

GRIMOALDO.

For someone else you well may have some fear.

RODELINDA.

What? You'd . . .

GRIMOALDO.

Go, say no more to bother me;

Quite soon enough you'll know what I decide.

Despite the efforts I have made for her,

The ingrate yet I tremble to displease;

And what I've offered that she has refused

Now hurts my virtue and betrays my love.

O duke, Unulfo is too credulous.

Too easily he formed so false a hope;

Make threats, since offers are just waste of time.

You who have flattered, come help me in pain.

Act III

ACT III. SCENE I.

GARIBALDO, RODELINDA.

GARIBALDO.

It's not now just the offer of a crown
A loving prince is making for your son,
And to which your refusal can seem due
Only to hate or magnanimity:
His life's at stake, and the deservèd rage
In which the lover's thrown by mother's scorn
Will punish by the blood of blameless son
The mother's so ungrateful hardened heart.
Consider now: the choice that's given you
Is to accept for him the crown or death.
His fate is in your hands: to love or scorn
Will let him reign or bring about his death.

RODELINDA.

Should I then need to make so great a choice,
I should be given time to think on it.

GARIBALDO.

You're given just a moment to decide:
I have my orders; and without delay,
Madame, you need to state your choice right now:
A word's soon said. If you wish that he die,

Pronounce the sentence, and I'll carry it
To execute the wishes of the king.
RODELINDA.
A word's soon said, but in so dire a case
Not soon does one see what word's to be said;
And either choice is so calamitous
That equal seems to me the pain of each.
Since now I must obey, bring here your lord.
GARIBALDO.
And what's your choice?
RODELINDA.
Oh, I shall let him know
That if . . .
GARIBALDO.
You first must tell your choice to me:
He's wearied now of your defiant speech;
And if I can't bear him assurance full
That your desires cohere to his hope,
His sight's an honor of which you're deprived.
RODELINDA.
What are you saying? Have I heard you well?
You fear thus that a woman, by complaints,
Might save the virtue that you try to take,
And might put back a hero 'midst his ilk

From which you'd take him by your foul advice?
Yes, I shall wed that master oh so blind,
Tyrannical as you force him to be:
Go, tell him then; but think about it twice.
Fear me, and fear his love, if he accepts.
I can do much o'er him; and even more,
Perhaps despite such bonds I'll reign one day.
GARIBALDO.
Yes, you will reign, Madame, and I'll be pleased
To nobly die for having served you well.
RODELINDA.
Go, I'll show him that services like yours
Deserve from him a cruel punishment,
And that for all the wrongs that kings may do,
Revenge is right on servants such as you.
While you await you can give him this joy,
That he to win my heart has found the track,
That his insulting zeal and your bad fate
Have paved the way for his so boorish love.
So tell him, if you must, I'm set to wed;
But flee us when it's done, fear for your life.
GARIBALDO.
I'll gladly give to you so great a king.

RODELINDA.

And so then let him pledge to me his faith.

SCENE II.

RODELINDA, EDUIGE.

EDUIGE.

Your happiness will have no guarantee

On basis of so short a span of time.

You have however quite impressive charms . . .

RODELINDA.

Well, I know secrets that you do not know;

And if my charms and worth are less than yours,

I've surer ways to rule out being left.

EDUIGE.

My case . . .

RODELINDA.

Permit that I not fear for it,

And by your own case do not judge of mine.

Each one at one's own risk must seek one's fate.

And I have cares that your case importunes.

EDUIGE.

I have no plan of importuning you.

RODELINDA.

Nor have I any plan to trouble you;

But, still, your jealousy so overwrought
Gives rise in me to feelings of unease.

EDUIGE.

I am not jealous; infidelity . . .

RODELINDA.

Well! Jealousy or curiosity,
Since when are we in such relationship
That my heart should be opened up to you?

EDUIGE.

I make no claim, and it's enough for me
To hear how your heart will accept a king.

RODELINDA.

One hears not always what one thinks one hears.

EDUIGE.

True, in a speech that's hard to understand,
I do not guess, and have no wit for it;
But wit's not needed where the ear's enough.

RODELINDA.

The ear would have to understand the thought.

EDUIGE.

I understand your thought: you have been forced;
Or threatened maybe with death of a son,
Or what a tyrant thinks allowed to him,
And then a weak excuse will make the rounds

To dazzle or deceive 'most everyone.
This heart however that you have left me . . .
RODELINDA.
It's not yet time for you to fret o'er it:
As he makes laws for me, do I for him.
EDUIGE.
He'll accept your laws lest he displease;
Accept his word, he keeps it oh so well.
RODELINDA.
To get back the throne one can risk all.
And let me have the glory or the shame,
Since only to myself must I account.
If your heart suffered as mine suffers now,
You'd find no pleasure in such interview;
And your soul seeing at that price a crown
Would wish in freedom to consult itself.
EDUIGE.
I beg your pardon if I cause you pain,
And I'll retire lest I cause you more.
RODELINDA.
Go, and persist with your confused mistake:
You don't deserve to have me set you straight.
EDUIGE.
The lover will address you without me,

And I need no more than my eyes' report.

SCENE III.

GRIMOALDO, RODELINDA, GARIBALDO, UNULFO.

RODELINDA.

Sir, I surrender now, but not to force:
The title that you take is bait for me,
And my affection's so well caught by it,
That only one condition does it seek:
If I could not love you when you were just,
When you're a tyrant I'll love you in crime;
Your marriage I'll regard as something good
If it bring infamy to you and me.

GRIMOALDO.

Why, Madam, I shall love an infamy
If it means you're no more my enemy!
Go on, go on, let's know the price at which
I'll put an end to your long-lasting scorn;
I wish one favor, you decide the rest.
I fear for Garibaldo fatal hate,
And for Unulfo too, please speak to that.

RODELINDA.

Go, bring that fear to hearts more déclassé;

I'd lower not myself to weakness such
As to seek vengeance 'gainst such petty souls.
If their bad counsels have forced me to reign,
I ought to hate them, and know how to scorn.
The heavens will choose for their punishment
Some lower means than my so noble hate.
But may they live, and may their grubbiness
In tyrant's shadow find security.
Just what I want from you now bears the sign
Of virtue that is worthy to please you.
Your offers lacked examples in the past,
And what I seek lacks precedent as well;
I wish it to provide a certain sign
That my son's interests now move me not,
That without thought of him will I be yours,
No thought of what he has to fear or hope.

GRIMOALDO.

Please finish overwhelming me with joy.
Now by what happy means must I trust you?
Explain yourself. I'll swear by skies above
To bring about quite soon our happiness.

RODELINDA.

So I'll obey and I'll explain myself.
From tyrant do I wish a tyrant's act:

And let the name of tyrant be deserved;
May all his virtue die with one big deed,
May he give up forever the bright signs
That placed him in the rank of worthy kings;
That he be seen as wicked, inhumane,
I wish by his own hand he kill my son.

GRIMOALDO.

My God!

RODELINDA.

What do you want for surer sign
Maternal thoughts have softened not my hate,
Without such thoughts I give myself to you,
No thoughts of what my son should fear or hope?
You shake, you're pale, it seems that you don't dare
To carry out what you propose to me!
If you need help, then I shall not draw back,
I'll lend you the example of my arm.
Have him brought here, that I kill him with you.
Though you withdraw your oath, I'll keep my word.
It's necessary that the crime unite
All that too many virtues kept apart.
Who's like a tyrant should indeed be one.
To fulfill the role must you be shown,
And must a mother by spilling of blood

Teach you to merit such a frightful name?
Do not allow the shame. Take all the fame
That to your memory will be attached.
And show your sycophants, who too much dare,
That you can tyrannize much more than I;
And by a deed that tyrants well may do,
Be tyrant over one who'd tyrannize.
Such is the price for which I give myself;
Or sell myself, if such word you'd prefer.
Consent to this price that your love gain me,
Since it will soil your fame as much as mine.

GRIMOALDO.

O Garibaldo, was that your report?

GARIBALDO.

'Twas with the jealous one she changed her mind;
I'd left her for the wedding fully set,
With nothing to suggest unpleasantness.
These furies after all are fantasy,
Intended to cause you confusion, lord;
Don't be surprised, you'll see a change of heart.

GRIMOALDO.

You order it, Madame. I must agree:
My victim he will be. I'm not averse
To see you be the first to strike a blow.

Whatever honor's joined then to my fame,
I want the glory to be shared with you,
And may posterity give me the blame
For having learned from you to tyrannize.
You ought to keep in check audacity,
And not give way to any show of rage,
To not permit of fury any hint,
That your deed not be seen to horrify.
To make a show of madness or despair,
Display outlandish abnormality,
To be outside yourself, thus demonstrate
The depths to which my love has brought you down,
Would be with too much art parade your pain;
The noisiest are not the sickest ones:
The great displeasures aren't most manifest;
One knows a great heart's always self-possessed.
And you know, Madam, that the greatest souls
Are not so low as to show feebleness,
And are not blinded unbecomingly;
That even their despair is rational,
And that . . .

RODELINDA.

Enough: a fair judge be of me,
Tell me if my despair is rational.

If I speak blindly, or if I see well.
You wish to give my son his heritage,
And all your virtue thereby goes away,
When you let me choose for him death or crown!
When I have satisfied your desp'rate vows,
Should I think that his life is more assured?
This offer or this gift of diadem
Is, to be frank, a feeble stratagem.
To make a child a king, to tutor be,
Is to pretend that one has not usurped;
It's choosing to be called by nicer name;
To be the sceptre's only arbiter,
And put a fantom on the throne as king
Till comes a son that's born to you from me,
Till they fear us, and till the time arrives
To place effective rule within his hands.
And who for his affection would kill him
Would gladly for ambition then kill him.
One can be tired soon of woman's love;
But thirst of reigning never leaves the soul;
And so as grandeur has eternal charms,
Our Italy's subject to sudden deaths.
There are ways to remove an obstacle,
And make a new king without miracle;

You can force yourself to heave some sighs,
And have the brow of one who is displeased.
Less open then the door to my revenge:
The fruit of his loss would I lose with him.
Since he must die, it's better soon than late;
May his death be by crime, and not by chance;
May his so blameless shade drive all my steps,
And endlessly demand a victim's head;
May this young king, who met death at your hand,
Make you abomination to all men;
May he excite great hatred far and wide;
May he make rebels all within this land.
I'll wed you then, yes I will force myself,
To better serve my hate and gain revenge,
To better fare against your barbary,
To be always the mistress of your life,
To have the way to push my fury forth,
And better choose the place to pierce your heart.
And there is my despair, and its just cause:
On these terms take my hand, if you do dare.

GRIMOALDO.

Oh yes, I take it, Madam, and I wish . . .

SCENE IV.

PERTARITO, GRIMOALDO, RODELINDA, GARIBALDO, UNULFO.

UNULFO.

But what, O lord? For Pertarito lives:
It's not a rumor, here he's being brought;
Some hunters found him in the nearby wood,
Where, hidden in a fort, he'd spend the night.

GRIMOALDO.

I see too clearly whose hand is at work.

RODELINDA.

Is it then you, lord? Have the faithless tongues
Spread only false reports about your fate?

PERTARITO.

Oh who, this spouse so dear to your desires,
Who has cost you so many tears and sighs . . .

GRIMOALDO.

Go, fantom, and rejoin who has sent you,
And meddle not to take away my joy.
There will be punishments enough for you,
If you show here the vain shade of a king.
For Pertarito's dead.

PERTARITO.

Oh no, he lives,

He speaks to you, he sees you in his lands.
May your ambition not be so afraid
As to imagine I'm not who I am:
It's shameful to pretend where one can do.
I'm dead if you wish, and dead if you dare,
That right to reign makes me deserve to die.
I come not here by any subterfuge
Intending to address my unjust fate,
To make use of assassins against you,
Or kill you for my great unhappiness.
Since fate has taken my birthright from me,
So much as to give you the pow'r I held,
Reign o'er my states that heaven's given you;
Perhaps another time will give back friends.
But please make better use of heaven's gift:
Don't take away my last remaining good,
A good to which I am a bar to you,
For which your wishes are iniquitous.
For Rodelinda's not part of your spoils:
Unless I'm killed, she can't belong to you.
Now that I'm found, my life depends on you;
As tyrant take it, or as king attack.
Even off the throne I bear its signs,
The throne that from my fathers came to me.

I wish that it suffice, despite your birth,
To give us both equality of rank.
If Rodelinda finds her soul's been charmed,
To see who merits her we need no troops.
I'm king, I am alone, and you thus can
By noble effort seek to gain your wish.

GRIMOALDO.

Such vulgar trick has no effect on me,
Eduige for that is not astute enough;
She's trained you badly, what skill she may have,
And too much fuss she's made about her plot.
She has destroyed the impact by the threat,
And led you to display bad grace, no more.

PERTARITO.

What? Do you really think that I've been hired?

GRIMOALDO.

So you'll admit yourself, by force or will.
One needs more secrecy, would one surprise,
And if one's been announced, there's no surprise.

PERTARITO.

Speak, Madam, speak, let it be seen by all
That you have eyes to recognize your spouse.

GRIMOALDO.

So I'm to heed one who's in league with you!

Well, speak now, Madam, carry out the plan.
Is he your spouse?

RODELINDA.

O you who wish to doubt,
With what confusion would you then ask me?
If you don't trust your eyes, will you trust me?
And don't you recognize him without me?
In battles you have seen him many times
Show, at your risk, his military skill,
And sword in hand dispute there for himself
Against you his right to his life and crown.
If to treat him as trickster you seek help,
Him who is king and husband to me still,
Ask Garibaldo, who beholds his lord:
One who'd betray him would deny him too;
And from his mortal fear you can receive
The answer that you will not get from me.
So high a service needs a lower soul;
You know . . .

GRIMOALDO.

Yes, I know well how far your boldness goes.
With hope to gain from my perplexity
You seek to see my spirit's been disturbed;
These speeches in the air your pride inspires

Wish to convey what you do not dare say,
To fool the people, so that they with you
Will treat the shameless fool as if your spouse.
Go further then, be more audacious still:
Tell us in full . . .

RODELINDA.

What would you have me say?
Your wish is that we say what you would hear:
Your sycophants accept what you decide.
But I can't say the things that you would hear;
And since his fate has placed him in your pow'r,
I know my duty, if you do him harm.
'Mong tyrants' ranks now cease to place yourself.

SCENE V.

GRIMOALDO, PERTARITO, GARIBALDO, UNULFO.

GRIMOALDO.

How all of this embarrasses me more!

GARIBALDO.

For such a trickster can you pity feel?

GRIMOALDO.

Oh no, a scaffold soon will end the ruse.
Let your rooms be used as a jail for him;

Unulfo, please guard him.

PERTARITO.

Prince, hear me out:

Countless witnesses will state my name;

Milan and Pavia . . .

GRIMOALDO.

Go now, no more:

You'll have full chance to make yourself be heard.

To Garibaldo.

And you, go see Eduige, and give to her

Some hope my love for her will be revived,

So that she then, believing in my pledge,

Will tell you who this faker really is.

SCENE VI.

GARIBALDO.

How unforeseen! How such a thunderclap

In just a moment can destroy my hopes!

Now this return, despite what I have planned,

Will send Grimoaldo back to his first goal;

And if as hero he now treats this prince,

Without a tyrant, I shall victim lack:

With nothing to avenge, I can't betray

If he's removed the ways to stir up hate.

Whatever happen now, let's not lose heart;
Let's force our lot to have a change of face;
Let's push Grimoaldo, for good of the state,
To treat him as a fake or fear a coup;
Let's fill his mind with terrifying thoughts
So he'll accept tyrannical advice;
Let's draw him back from virtuous display,
That Pertarito find himself undone.
Perhaps Eduige, who might feel some regret,
Won't accept him stained with brother's blood,
And thus our claim will finally win out
Both as to love and to ambition too.
Let's try at least, whatever happen now,
And do all that we can to reign one day.

Act IV

ACT IV. SCENE I.

GRIMOALDO, GARIBALDO.

GARIBALDO.

I still say to you, lord, this prompt return
Is but a trick that's made to thwart your love.
So I deduce from all that Eduige said:
She was afflicted by your change of heart,
And with this trickster who's like the late king,
In her despair she makes a final try.
And Rodelinda too would give you pain:
One serves her love, the other serves her hate;
What one produced, the other vouches for,
And in complicity they would fool you.
The faker yet, whate'er he's asked to feign,
Better plays the role with naught to fear;
Be it that his speeches so move you
That you give to Eduige what she first sought;
Be it that Rodelinda 'spite the trick
Retain the power that she holds o'er you,
To neither one can your disordered soul
Deny the pardon that is sought from you.

GRIMOALDO.

True, Garibaldo, and, yes, I shall give

My crown to which of them would share with me:
Not that I hope to soften still that rock
That neither my respect nor vows have swayed.
If I loved Rodelinda, loved but her,
My soul broke faith with her who loved but me;
If eternal scorn and discontent
Bravado, hate, the mess in which I am,
Have been till now the only recompense
Of that so wrongful love my heart has felt,
It's time henceforth that by a good attempt
I free my heart from that unworthy fate.
Let's seize the chance Eduige has given us:
Let's love the trick to which her love's been forced.
Eduige laments an ingrate who's known woes
And lends a hand to free him from his chains.
Let's love, again I say, the stratagem,
Let's love its help and do it justice now.
Be it she wants the throne or wants but me,
Be it she loves Grimoaldo or the king,
Be it from love or courage that she acts,
I owe all to the hand that sets me free.
O you who to obey me spoke with her,
To try to make her feel but hate for me,
O Duke, no more, now bring to her my word:

That to her fires I repay what I stole,
And that thus with a single action I
Can honor her ambition and her love.

GARIBALDO.

As you say, sir; but finally beware
Of what new risks that effort might create,
And if it isn't to trust all too soon
The fleeting feeling that has come to life.
The faker then will be passed off as king:
Your kindness people then will take as sign;
And ardently then in his new found place
Respected he will think his rank to be.
I know that soon your bravery so great
Will tame the rashness of the mutineers;
But are you very sure what to expect
From Eduige to whom you'd surrender self?
Lord, I have looked quite deeply in her soul,
Where I've seen little trace of love for you:
Her hatred acts and seeks to take from you
What all your wishes try to carry off.
She wants, it's true, to call you back towards her;
But to be thankless, to be cruel herself,
To treat you badly and pay back to you
Her own bad faith for yours, and scorn for scorn.

She wants your soul, become a slave to hers,
To seek but never to obtain her grace:
Those are her very words; to harm you more,
She wants to love me, all within your sight:
So has she said.

SCENE II.

GRIMOALDO, GARIBALDO, EDUIGE.

EDUIGE.

So have I said, you snake!
Yes, so I said, and might have done perhaps,
If your soul, which was bound to my commands,
Had shown itself quite capable of love.
My secrets did I tell in confidence!
Grimoaldo, see from that your wisdom's lack,
And judge then from my secrets so disclosed
Just how secure yours told to him will be.
One who betrays a mistress makes it known
That he'd betray a master just the same,
And, with his faith then floating 'twixt the two,
No love feels he for master or for me.
He has a goal, Grimoaldo, so beware:
Whatever be his plan, he watches you.
So look within that heart and judge it well.

One who'd betray my love seeks higher things.
GARIBALDO.
Oh how unfairly, lord, you can now see
My services for you she deems a crime.
But what might not unhappy lover do
When he has constant fear of losing you,
Madame? You wish the king you to adore,
And to prevent that I'd do even more:
I won't prevent myself, my jealousy
Seeks every way to distance him from you.
I'd not bear seeing you in other arms;
My love, if it be crime, resembles yours.
What would not you do to make the king
Leave Rodelinda for his pledge to you?
And just what here has not been put in play
By your excessive boldness and your zeal?
I've made great efforts to belong to you;
But nothing can I do to wake the dead.
I've spoken truths of which your heart has hummed:
Imposture, though, I never would approach,
And I've not uttered sentiments so fine
As to release the shadows from their tombs.
'Twas not my love brought Pertarito here:
My flame knows not the art for such a deed;

In my love there is nothing to be blamed,
Unless to love's the same as to betray.

EDUIGE.

Of what am I accused by one so rude?

GRIMOALDO.

Of feeble unsuccessful stratagem.
Ma'am, badly put together is your plan:
The revelation came as no surprise.
You yourself had forewarned me of it,
And, warned, I thus expected it to come.
Console yourself, it has made its effect:
I'm yours, Madame, and yes, completely so.
I've been untrue, and if my fickle heart
Has stolen from you what was due to you,
If I had turned my thoughts to someone else,
The ills I've suffered have well punished me.
I see well now, and recognize my crime:
My fires relit, to you I give this heart;
Yes, princess, to be yours until the end,
It asks a pardon it does not deserve.
Your kindness if it should make the request
Gains the fake Pertarito pardon too.
Such tentative wounds kingly majesty;
But if it's criminal, so I've been too.

Be gracious, as am I; let's both forget.
His public declaration's needed now,
By truthful statement that leaves nothing out,
That he tried to trick me on your behalf,
And that he made his claim at your command.
Madame, thus be assured you'll share my crown,
And don't allow this trick in any way
To help potential mutiny 'gainst us.
So have him then confess; my pardon will
Allow th'impostor to reveal himself;
And thereby free from these disturbing things
The sceptre that your hands and mine will hold.
EDUIGE.
I had till now for your fame some respect,
That calling you a tyrant seemed so strange:
And like a suspect I felt that my fire
Made secret disavowal of the charge:
But you unmask, my scruple goes away.
No longer can I keep respect for you;
And I see clearly, now the mask is gone,
That never was a tyrant more complete.
Adroitly do you play soft and severe,
To have a sister 'gainst her brother act:
And more, you wish that he betray his fate,

Blame self, and hand self over to his death,
As if he could be so in love with life
As to redeem it by ignominy,
Or that a hope to see you back with me
Could make me just as faithless as you are.
Love me in my disloyalty, but don't
Expect me to help cause my brother's death.
If I spoke of his possible return,
If I alarmed you for your newfound love,
It wasn't airy talk that I made up
To blur the minds of you and of his wife.
I wanted to harm you, and spoke by chance,
At least to cause some future harm to you;
And when by his return he stunned us all,
The heavens gave me more than I had hoped.

GRIMOALDO.

Madame . . .

EDUIGE.

You waste time; I will hear no more.
I await your choice, to make my own.
Act, if you wish, with magnanimity;
Or act as tyrant, and so take a life:
I'll follow your example, by your choice
I'll show my hatred or my tenderness.

It is enough I disabuse you now,
As payment for your love or for your ruse.
Good-bye.

SCENE III.
GRIMOALDO, GARIBALDO, UNULFO.
GRIMOALDO.
Unulfo?
UNULFO.
I must tell you now
Some people have been coming to see him.
But only a few visits I allowed;
As Pertarito they acknowledged him.
The common people speak of him, and now
One hears confusèd rumors here and there . . .
GARIBALDO.
Oh see what risks the faker makes for you:
The people speak and murmur 'mongst themselves.
A fire will be lit, if it's not stopped.
To get rid of that man, what can you fear?
The hatred of Eduige, who offers you
But savage pride as her only response?
She whom your shows of scorn, which maddened her,
Now make you hesitate to make mistakes?

Yes, she whose only thirst is for your loss?
Yes, whose hand alone drives this machine?
Oh, such misfortunes ought to be disdained,
And timid virtue is not fit to reign.
Wed Rodelinda, and despite the ghost,
Secure the state and make the kingdom calm;
Delivering the faker to his fate,
Remove today all pretext for revolt.

GRIMOALDO.

Yes, I agree; tomorrow then his head,
Slain at my feet, will put to rest the storm.
Have him brought here, and send along with him
The one who's his supporter number two,
The queen who flouts me and who seems to be
Reluctant yet to call herself his wife.

GARIBALDO.

Her tears will move you.

GRIMOALDO.

Against them I'm armed.

GARIBALDO.

You'll be seduced by love.

GRIMOALDO.

I've no such fear;
No strength has love when my soul is resolved.

GARIBALDO.

Act then, my lord, with power absolute:
Sustain your sceptre with th' authority
That majesty imprints on brows of kings.
A king must power have, and is no king
When he allows another rule his heart.

SCENE IV.

GRIMOALDO, PERTARITO, RODELINDA, GARIBALDO, UNULFO.

GRIMOALDO.

Experience my kindness, faker, come,
And don't reduce it to severity.
I want to pardon you: so now confess
Who led you to take part in such a plan,
Who formed it, and who taught you what to do:
You hear me; put to end this false report;
Instruct my subjects, open is your jail;
If not, tomorrow you will meet your death;
Don't force your prince, let stubbornness be gone,
Deserve the pardon that he wants to give.

PERTARITO.

How you are using ruse and artifice
To simulate of justice a display,

And save the semblance of the rectitude
With which you try to clothe yourself again!
A victim great has heaven given you,
To see if magnanimity you'll show;
But all that heaven lets you take is blood,
And not the victim's name or victim's rank.
I'll die as king, one born to wear the crown;
And soon my subjects, no more fooled by you,
Will know by my death that they see in you
False colors that depict you as a king.
So hasten then my death, which you so need;
For since you want to hear the truth sincere,
The only wishes that I'm forming now
Are to free soon my people from their woe.
Fear me if I escape; 'twill be your loss
If opened up to me's the prison door.
My people will have eyes to see their king,
And tell between a tyrant and their king:
Such fury will I then excite in them.
Know Pertarito's hope though he's in chains;
See all the truths he cannot hide from you,
And his avowal to enlighten you.
RODELINDA.
Now do you wish to see yet nobler signs?

To see the blood of our forefather kings?
This heart so great . . .

GRIMOALDO.

Yes, Madam, he's well taught
To show some pride and make a royal show.
But if avowal, made by his own words,
Does not set right the people's views today,
Let him prepare his head, and you yourself
Bid him good-bye for all eternity.
Let's leave the two; Unulfo, you stand guard;
Let no one come or go till I say so.

SCENE V.

PERTARITO, RODELINDA.

PERTARITO.

Madame, you see where love's conducted me.
I knew there were false stories of my death,
And of the tyrant's wishes I had heard;
I feared where his desires were to lead,
And felt therefore I must expose myself,
To see you once again and set you straight.
And so I put at risk, with such a plan,
The sad remains of my unwelcome life,
To which, apart from you, the tedium

Seemed always on the verge of snuffing out;
For, I'll admit, in such a sorry state
Where hatred of my fate had brought me low,
Where all my allies turned away from me,
Most deeply I bemoaned not seeing you.
I bless my fate, whatever ills it send,
Since it allows this little time of joy;
And though it dares betray me once again,
For such a time so sweet I cannot hate.

RODELINDA.

So little was it, lord, for my sad soul,
Of all the woe in which I had been plunged;
So little were the rigors of my jail,
Without that to which your love had thrown you;
And as a last outrage he gives to me,
I'll see you die and know that I'm the cause!
I won't say that I find this moment sweet.
Too high's the price for what it gives of you;
Your memory would have defended me
From all a tyrant would have dared to claim.
No sighs or tears should you expect from me:
They are amusements meant for lighter woes.
The love I have for you hates such soft depths
From which a fearful sex's weakness comes;

I've strengthened self too much against such woes
To not disdain the use of any sigh.
The noble feelings of displeasure such
Will turn themselves to ardor for revenge,
And scorning show, will make every attempt
To save your life, or to avenge your death.
I will do one of those, or die myself.
PERTARITO.
Love rather, Madam, conqu'ror who loves you.
You've done enough for me, and for your fame;
It's time to seek the side of happiness,
And to embrace no more sad destinies,
And to allow my days and woes to end.
The heavens, who meant you to rule herein,
Grant me the boon of dying before you.
I love to see them break an unsought chain
Of which the breaking makes you happy queen;
And 'neath your fate I wish well to succumb
To put back in your hands what I'd made fall.
RODELINDA.
Is that then, lord, the worthy recompense
For constancy I've shown to your sad shade?
When I thought you were dead, the vanquisher,
His conquest at my feet, then sought my heart,

When others in my place might deem it good,
An homage coming from his victory . . .
PERTARITO.
I know that you've combatted laudably:
Your virtue surely heaven's going to crown;
And it will free you from anxiety
That could have come from doubts about my death,
And will set you at ease with liberty
To have the highest kind of happiness.
RODELINDA.
What say you, spouse?
PERTARITO.
That I can calmly see
Your happiness spring from my sad events.
Love brought me back, unable to do more
Than wrap you in the exile of a spouse,
To take away from you the vicious zeal
Where my life and my wife's name were opposed.
To change with honor, you will need my death;
And if 'twill let you reign, it's not in vain.
And after all your woes that my love caused,
It's time that my death be of use to you,
And that a victor prostrate at your feet
Cease to relinquish all of his virtue.

Of a conqu'ror so great, a hero rare,
You've made too long a tyrant or a brute,
Though be he one for crushing your rebuffs.
Be his, Madame; he'll be a brute no more;
And happily shall I have lost my life,
Since . . .

RODELINDA.

Finish not a speech that's killing me,
And force me not to die of sorrow now,
Before I've ended or avenged your woes.
Yes, I who scorned him in his victory,
Magnanimous, brave, just, good, generous,
To join the shade of one disconsolate,
I could within your sight, at your life's cost,
Wed the tyrant's dreadful infamy,
Betray my honor and my birth and rank,
To kiss a hand still fuming with your blood!
Ah! Better you should know me, husband dear.

PERTARITO.

No need to have such scruple in your soul.
While common duties are beset with laws,
The throne dispenses kings from such concerns:
Their glory is above the common rules
And not subject to rules for vulgar hearts.

For once a vanquished king's in victor's hands,
Too well does he deserve to end his life.
My death for Grimoaldo can't be crime:
For strengthening his reign makes all allowed.
When I'm no longer breathing in his chains,
Give him your hand, with no more thoughts to weigh:
Spare efforts of a hate that's powerless,
And let the heavens make you queen again.
RODELINDA.
Oh spare me, lord, this cruel sentiment.
For well you know . . .

SCENE VI.
PERTARITO, RODELINDA, UNULFO.
UNULFO.
Madame, please finish now:
The king, becoming willful more and more,
Calls for this prince, be he prince true or false.
PERTARITO.
So I must say farewell; believe a spouse
Has all the feelings he should have for you.
He sees your love and all that you deserve;
It's leaving you, not dying, he regrets.

RODELINDA.

So I must say farewell; and take my word
That I'll be worthy both of you and me.

PERTARITO.

Be not exposed to the same precipice.

RODELINDA.

Oh, heaven, hating tyrants, will be just.

PERTARITO.

Were it so just, it would have granted you
A stronger monarch, not one out of luck.

Act V

ACT V. SCENE I.

UNULFO, EDUIGE.

EDUIGE.

Grimoaldo still insists my brother die!
He treats his sorry state as just a trick!
And feigning to give me his heart and faith,
He has no eyes for him or ears for me!

UNULFO.

Ma'am, blame the duke who has a hold on him:
The harm, if he's believed, will have no cure;
And if the king took his inflamed advice,
You'd see already its blood-soaked effects.

EDUIGE.

He left my brother for Grimoaldo's side;
He fears his payment if my brother lives.

UNULFO.

Add that he loves you, and by any means
Would keep that victor to his former links;
And wishes Rodelinda to assure
Eternal separation 'twixt you two;
And if he manages to bring it off,
By force or love he thinks he will gain you.

But you, my lady, have no cause to fear;
The hero's yours without reserve or feint.
And . . .
EDUIGE.
If he leaves the one he cherished so,
It must be that her husband he does know.
But if, despite the traitor, he knew him,
Who'd stop him then from making him appear?
UNULFO.
He fears attack against the throne he's won,
And for reasons of state denies the truth.
A necessary blindness, so he's thought;
As Garibaldo stirred his ire up,
Combatted always by his bad advice,
He creates doubts as to his probity.
But, madam, things are not now as they were.
I've seen so long this peril to his fame.
Whatever fruit the duke to gather hopes,
I've taken from the king the means to act.
No more is Pertarito in his pow'r.
But think not that I have been so unwise
As to give to his flight th'ability
To show himself to rouse the people's hearts.
I've lent a hand to let him safely flee,

Or rather faithful escort did I give,
Which under the appearance of support
Removes him from the realm and lets me know.
I thus prevent the work the duke had planned,
And as a hostage give the king my head.
Your kindness, madam, will take care of it.
EDUIGE.
Yes, I'll do what it takes, should there be need:
I'll take the blame, if that's what I must do.
UNULFO.
Unless I do not know his virtue well,
When he's back to himself, he'll be so pleased
As to be first to say I served him well.

SCENE II.
GRIMOALDO, EDUIGE, UNULFO.
GRIMOALDO.
What do you wish, Madame, that I expect?
What do you want from me?
EDUIGE.
What are your plans?
What sentence for my brother will there be?
GRIMOALDO.
For an impostor still you have concerns?

EDUIGE.

Wish you to take tyrannical advice
From one who'd give you o'er to public hate?

GRIMOALDO.

And for the wrongful fake you would blame me!
The mercy that I've offered you've refused.

EDUIGE.

That offer's penalty to one oppressed;
No mercy needs there be where there's no crime;
Your eyes, despite yourself, can't fail to see
That mercy's his to grant and not to get.
Be not so stubborn as to blind yourself:
Be as I loved you, if you want my love;
Be as you seemed when you subdued Milan:
The conqueror I love, the tyrant not.
Regain that virtue, full, and high, sincere,
Which strengthened you upon my brother's throne;
Give him his name, if you give me your heart.
One who can feign for him can feign for me;
In me you see a lover unconvinced
When I see how your soul is false with him.
Renounce a tyrant's virtues as true king,
And hide no more the heart you give to me.

GRIMOALDO.

So read in it yourself: it's yours, Madame;
You see the trouble as well as the flame.
And without asking what indeed you know,
Believe of it, please, all that you do think.
It's to redouble my ills and my shame,
To force my mouth to render you account.
Had I no eyes, each man has eyes for me.
Lone Garibaldo has denied his king;
And by an interest, seen easily,
My hand he'd use for Pertarito's death.
But heaven strike me dead before your eyes
If I should think to spill such precious blood!
But, Madam, put yourself within my place:
If him I recognize, what do I then?
Keep him in chains who bears the name of king,
Is to arouse his people against me.
Or set him free, that puts him at their head,
Thus hastening myself the coming storm.
Can I with safety permit his return?
Can I sit on his throne with him at court?
A king, although deposed, retains mystique:
His faithful subjects still revere his sight;
When he appears, the greatest conquerors,

However virtuous, as tyrants seem:
His presence wakens deep within their hearts
A secret feeling he their master is.
My fate thus has what for to punish me,
To set him free, and to keep him locked up.
I see his person in my prisons kept
More to be feared than at an army's head.
For there my arm, by valor energized,
Would seek with glory to pierce his heart;
But here, without defense! What can I do?
For me to reign, I need that he be dead;
But suddenly his virtue arms him well,
To give him more support than many troops.
To save his life and maintain my empire,
I do what I can do to deny him:
And of cruel tyrants I put on the rage,
To get avowals from the queen and you;
But everywhere I waste my time, because
Resistance is what all my efforts meet.
Still if there were no need to kill or scorn
Amid troubles so great that spoil my reign,
And if to love you and displease you not,
Unnecessary were the rank of king,
If I defeat myself, give him the state,

I'd show my virtue in a brighter light.
But I lose you if I give up the crown;
Since you require a king, it's you I lose;
And in this heart you know has fought for you,
To all my virtue all my love's opposed.
You for whom I'm blind midst so much light,
If you still pay attention to my prayers,
Please deign to guide me in my lack of sight,
Yes, for a brother's and a lover's sake.
My love for both makes you the sovereign:
Please order them youself and speak as queen.
I'll die content, and all will seem so sweet,
Provided that you think that I am yours.
EDUIGE.
How badly you know me, my brother too!
You think the crown's so very dear to me
That I dare to disdain a gen'rous count
To join myself unto a tyrant's fate?
Please love me if you wish, but think me kind:
With all that love, preserve esteem for me;
Believe my feelings for my own true blood.
Believe I love my virtue more than rank,
And that I deem your oath had been fulfilled
Before you reigned here for a single day.

Milan, who saw him flee and named you king,
From hatred of a dead man has freed me.
I am free now, and as a lover true
I help your wav'ring virtue despite you,
And save my brother from your thirst to rule,
Before your heart's been won by such a thirst.
Oh yes, I broke his chains, I bribed his guards,
I put in safety all that you would risk.
He flees, and you've no more to treat as fake
The fearful author of your secret woes.
He flees, and you've no more a storm to fear.
And by my help, your conquest is assured;
And all the care I took . . .   But here's the queen.

SCENE III.

GRIMOALDO, RODELINDA, EDUIGE, UNULFO.

GRIMOALDO.

To Rodelinda

You're late, Madame. What care has held you back?
Pursue your husband's name, image, or shade;
Increase the number of those false to me,
And free my eyes, too easily they're charmed,
From risk of seeing and of loving you.
Go on: your captive's captive you're no more.

RODELINDA.

Give him to me, that I may follow him.
To what unworthy trick dare you to run,
To open up his cell when he is dead!
O sneak, think you that rumor of his flight
Will hide the savage conduct of your ire?
Think you there are no eyes to see your deeds
And see within your heart your many wrongs?

EDUIGE.

Madame . . .

RODELINDA.

Accomplice then to him are you?
Will you take on the blame for what's been done?
And do you like his hand at such a price?

EDUIGE.

And yet you wished him stained with your son's blood,
And I can take him stained with brother's blood,
A sister such as you a mother were.

RODELINDA.

Do not blame me for fury justified
To which I was reduced by tyrant's fire;
And since it seems his faith you have regained,
Cease then the bitterness of jealousy.

EDUIGE.

Do not blame me for jealous sentiments,
When I hate tyrants just as much as you.

RODELINDA.

You hate them when you have Grimoaldo's love!

EDUIGE.

I love his virtue more than any crown;
And seeing now what motives make him act,
I see in him no reason I should blush.

RODELINDA.

Blush then yourself, yes you who hide your crime,
You who, killing a king, your victim hide,
Disguising thus the fate of a great foe,
With claim he lied in life and fled in death.
All your false virtues' brilliant practices

Have elevated no great tombs for you;
They were vain shows of generosity,
Meant to increase your fame at little price.
You overwhelmed his name with fun'ral rites
To bury in obscurity his death,
And set for him with pomp so fine a trap,
Thus to deprive him one day of a tomb.
Be sated with his blood; give me what's left,
While justice or my vengeance you await,
So that . . .

GRIMOALDO.

To what now do you reduce me
All for a fake you wish to call your spouse?
Your pity only serves to give me shame,
If when you take him, I must give account,
And if the cruelty of my sad fate
Names me the killer of the one you save.

UNULFO.

My lord, I think I know the route he took;
And if her majesty wants me to go,
At my life's risk, within an hour or two,
I will return to her the one she seeks.
Let's go, let's go, Madame, and let me try . . .

RODELINDA.
O you base tyrant's baser minister,
Who 'neath a false pretense of decency
Imagine you've an answer for my tears!
Why not say rather that his just alarm
Would hide my tears from his good subjects' eyes,
And that I must be banned, for fear my cries
Should stir up common folk, and courtiers too?
O traitor, were you not in league with him,
Could he decline reprisal against you?
Grimoaldo, all your anger, where's it now?
Your orders placed my husband 'neath his guard.
He broke his chains and knows where he has fled;
And if I wish, he would take me to him;
And when his blood should be the price he pays,
He sees and speaks to you, and nothing fears!
GRIMOALDO.
When what he does for you would risk my life,
I cannot punish him for serving you.
If I however had fear that your cries
Would stir up common folk, and courtiers too,
With no need to request that you should flee,
Full many means have I to hide your tears.
But, Madam, you are at full liberty;

You can take action now with all your pride,
To take to ev'ry heart what's in your soul:
The husband's conqu'ror cannot fear the wife.
What does that soldier want?

SCENE IV.

GRIMOALDO, PERTARITO, RODELINDA, EDUIGE, UNULFO, SOLDIER.

SOLDIER.

To Grimoaldo.

To tell you, Lord,
Of two things, one unhappy and one sad.
No more lives Garibaldo, and the fake
Who poses here as king just loosed his soul;
But this same fake is in your power now.

GRIMOALDO.

What do you say?

SOLDIER.

Just what you're going to see.

GRIMOALDO.

O heavens! How my fortune is reduced
If I can't take advantage of his flight!
Must once again my so embarrassed heart
The power lack . . . But tell us what took place.

SOLDIER.

The duke, who'd been informed of the reports
A certain fake had from your justice fled,
Awaited him with men, and barred the way.
He told us, "Take him, but without a wound.
Preserve his blood for punishment to come.
Allow all those escorting him to flee."
The men who led him, suddenly surprised,
Surrounded then by those who'd come with me,
Accept the situation that they face,
And from false Pertarito move away.
He, whom the order to us was to spare,
And not to draw our swords to threaten him,
In desperation makes his way through us,
Up to our chief to vent to him his rage,
And plunges thrice a dagger in his breast,
Before any of us had kenned his plan.
Our arms were raised to smite him on the spot;
The duke, however, told us to refrain,
And with his last breath ordered us again
To save his blood for punishment to come.
And thus the fugitive is back in chains,
My lord, for you to name his penalty.
And here he is.

GRIMOALDO.

To go through this again!

SCENE V.

GRIMOALDO, PERTARITO, RODELINDA, EDUIGE.

PERTARITO.

O tyrant, once again you see me here;
And I have paid for you a service rare,
The one who sends me back to your false court.
Weep for that arm that had served you so well;
Weep for the one my arm just took from you.
Now hasten to seek vengeance for his death:
Your vengeance that he called for as he died.
Display your love, and show yourself today,
If he was worthy, worthier than he.
But cease to treat as any kind of fake
The traits that nature pressed upon my brow.
Milan saw me go by, and everywhere
I saw tears shed for the now helpless prince;
In vain you would disguise your tyranny:
Push as far as it goes your insolence;
Whatever sentence you prescribe for me,
Now end my days as the days of a king.

GRIMOALDO.

Yes, king you are, indeed, and I have known
So from the moment when I first saw you.
If I have shut my eyes and twisted things,
I wished to free you from int'rests of state,
And not permit my glory be undone
By any need to sacrifice your life.
The cultivation of such blindness then
Gave me persona of one driven mad,
And forced my virtue to embrace a game
To rob you of your name by fear of death.
But then my plan was only to affright
Or to oblige someone to help you leave.
Unulfo understood, so faithful he,
Just what I had expected from his zeal;
Oh, but a traitor pressed by other thoughts
Destroyed the goal I'd secretly desired.
Your hand, thank God, has done justice to him.
However your return pains me again;
For what do you wish that I do with you?
Can I treat you as king and keep the throne?
Could all your loving people look at you
And let another master make the laws?
Could you without putting in place a plan

Behold me as possessor of your goods?
And if the opportunity arrives,
Could you refuse a plot to end my life?
If you were but a coward, one could hope
That you could live and take no steps 'gainst me;
But one who dares defy me openly,
However weak he be, has no slave's heart,
And shows amidst misfortune a great soul
That may lack fortune but lacks valor not.
Despite myself I see that I'm required
To give you back your throne or take your life;
The more ambition agitates my thoughts,
The more my virtue will not let you die.
Imprisoning my virtue is too much:
I owe it freedom as I do to you;
Though my ambition well may be displeased,
My virtue triumphs, and so you will reign.
Milan, behold your prince, your master true,
Whom vainly I refused to recognize;
And you whom I had treated as a fake . . .
PERTARITO.
Too far you carry generosity.
Make Rodelinda mine, and keep my crown,
That for her freedom I am glad to cede:

With my belovèd my fate will be sweet.
GRIMOALDO.
The queen, Milan, and all my heart are yours;
And I'd return all Lombardy to you
If Pavia I ruled as you rule here.
You know not, lord, that Pavia's late king
Had made Eduige its queen; and on my oath
I swore . . .
EDUIGE.
If oath make you defend my throne,
More reason then have I to give it you;
And I would well deserve a change again,
If my heart equalled not my lover's heart.
PERTARITO.
Oh, his example you evoke in vain.
For Pavia I leave to you and him,
And I would deem myself unfortunate
If without sceptre I saw arm so good.
RODELINDA.
Forgive me if my hate seemed all too true:
For from your fury much did I presume;
But I would have never dared to presume
That in the end you'd force me to love you.

GRIMOALDO.

Your outrage was no injustice to me.

RODELINDA.

Oh, may firm friendship join us all today,

May our two states admire their joint links,

And doubt with cause which of you two does reign.

PERTARITO.

So that these fortunate events be known,

Let's call attention to what has transpired,

And show our people, happily surprised,

That for high virtue glory is the prize!!

THE END

About the translator

John R. Pierce studied French literature at Harvard, and law at Boston College. He has previously translated Corneille's *Cinna, or The Clemency of Augustus*, and *Attila, King of the Huns*.

John R. Pierce

https://twitter.com/jrpierce